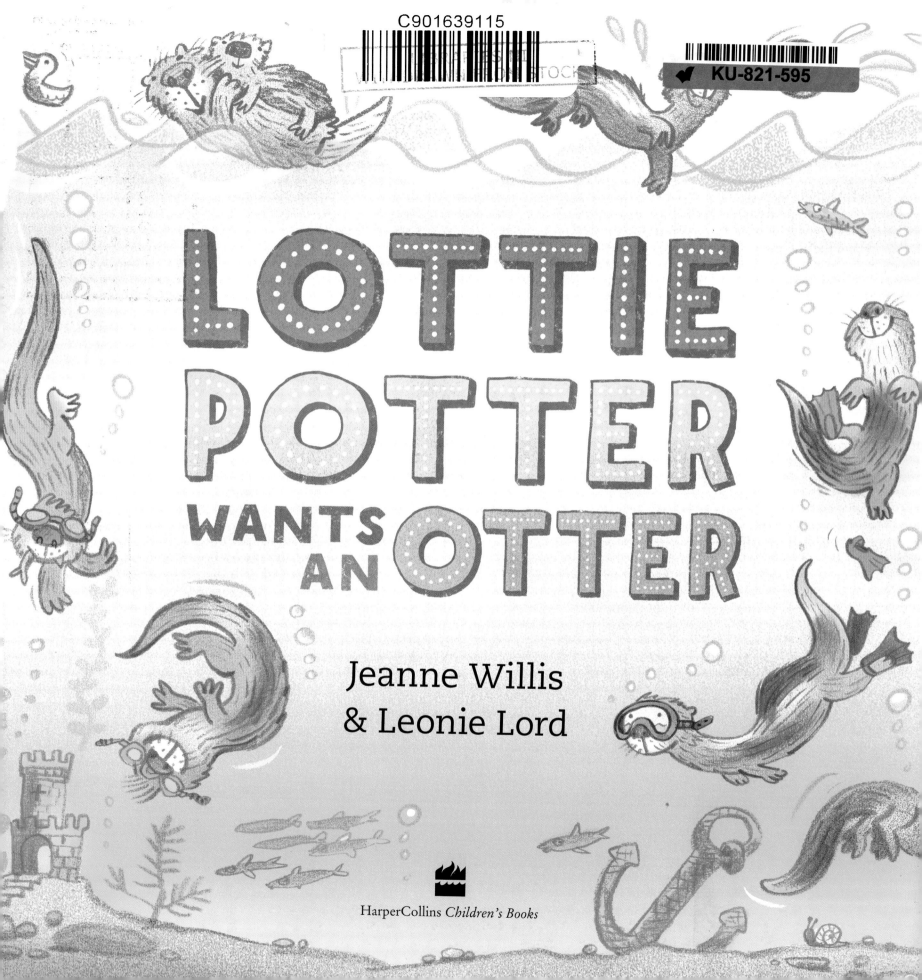

LOTTIE POTTER WANTS AN OTTER

Jeanne Willis
& Leonie Lord

HarperCollins Children's Books

"I really want an otter!"

uttered little Lottie Potter...

So off she tottered down to Tilly Town.
With a skip and with a hop,

she stopped at Trotter's Otter Shop
to look for something furry, warm and brown.

"Good morning, Mr Trotter,
I would like to buy an otter,"
		said little Lottie Potter, "if you please."

"What sort of otter, Lottie? I've got **lots**," said Mr Trotter.

"I've got these

and these

and

these...

...and these... and these!"

"I've got **spotty** otters,

potty otters,

hot from Lanzarote otters,

otters, every **shape** and every **size.**

I've got
snotty
otters,

swotty
otters,

tangled-in-a-**knotty**
otters…

...otter kits in cots with dots for eyes."

"My goodness, Mr Trotter,
you have got a lot of otters!" muttered Lottie.
"It is very hard to choose.

I'd forgotten that these creatures
had so many different features
from the otters that they keep in all the zoos."

"I've got otters out the back
in pink and purple, blue and black,"

said Mr Trotter. "Would you like to have a peek?"

"I've got **stinky** otters,

slinky otters,

swimming-in-the-**sinky** otters.

Otters that can **sing and dance and** squeak."

"Which do you suggest?"
said Lottie. "Which would be the best?
Because I'm not an otter expert, I'm afraid."

"Take this little chappy," Trotter said,
"he'll make you happy."

So Lottie got her purse out
and she paid.

But...

The otter that he got her

was a
bounder

and a rotter...

It was grumpy,

it was grotty...

...and it **bit** poor pretty little Lottie

very hard upon the **botty**...

and it didn't give a **jot** it hurt to sit.

She caught the naughty otter
and she brought it back to Trotter,

but the Otter Shop was shut
and up for sale.

It seemed that Mr Trotter
had got shot of all his otters
and retired to a caravan in Wales.

So little Lottie Potter
took a yacht across the water
and released the rotten otter in Phuket
where it instantly forgot her...

...but poor little Lottie Potter
was still positively pining for a pet.

So...

"I'm looking for a beaver!"
she announced to Mrs Cleaver
at the Beaver Stall in Tilly Market Square...

But the beavers were such *divas*,
and as much as it might grieve us...

Lottie changed her mind and bought...

...a Grizzly Bear!

For Lucian Bridgewood – J.W. x
For Eliza – L.L.

First published in paperback in Great Britain by HarperCollins Children's Books in 2016

1 3 5 7 9 10 8 6 4 2

ISBN: 978-0-00-750133-5

HarperCollins Children's Books is a division of HarperCollins Publishers Ltd.

Text copyright © Shakespeare's Monkey Limited 2016
Illustrations copyright © Leonie Lord 2016

Visit our website at: www.harpercollins.co.uk

Printed in China